ANITA BLAKE

The Laughing Corpse

NECROMANCER

ANITA BLAKE

The Laughing Corpse

NECROMANCER

WRITER . . . . LAURELL K. HAMILTON

ADAPTATION . . . . JESS RUFFNER

ART . . . . RON LIM

COLORS . . . . JOEL SEGUIN & LAURA VILLARI

LETTERS . . . . BILL TORTOLINI

COVER ART . . . . RON LIM, JAKE BILBAO & HARVEY TOLIBAO

EDITOR . . . . MICHAEL HORWITZ

SENIOR EDITOR . . . . RALPH MACCHIO

SPECIAL THANKS TO JONATHON GREEN,
MELISSA MCALISTER, ANNE TREDWAY & MARK PANICCIA

COLLECTION EDITOR . . . . CORY LEVINE

ASSISTANT EDITOR . . . . ALEX STARBUCK

ASSOCIATE EDITOR . . . . JOHN DENNING

EDITORS, SPECIAL PROJECTS . . . . JENNIFER GRÜNWALD & MARK D. BEAZLEY

SENIOR EDITOR, SPECIAL PROJECTS . . . . JEFF YOUNGQUIST

SENIOR VICE PRESIDENT OF SALES . . . . DAVID GABRIEL

SENIOR VICE PRESIDENT OF STRATEGIC DEVELOPMENT . . . . . RUWAN JAYATILLEKE

BOOK DESIGN . . . . SPRING HOTELING

EDITOR IN CHIEF . . . . JOE QUESADA

PUBLISHER . . . . DAN BUCKLEY

NECROMANCER

The morally absent —and mob-connected— businessman Harold Gaynor offered vampire hunter and animator Anita Blake one million dollars to raise a three-centuries-old corpse. She turned him down, but a visit from Harold's bodyguard made it clear he won't take no for an answer.

Anita found another enemy in Dominga Salvador, a voodoo priestess who wanted more than Anita was willing to give in exchange for helping her find a missing boy. In return, Dominga promised that something would come to hurt Anita when she least expects it.

The boy's corpse is discovered, mutilated by what Anita believes to be a superhumanly strong zombie. Anita swears to find the undead killer—and the mysterious animator powerful enough to raise it.

Between all of this and a run-in with the new master vampire of St. Louis, Jean-Claude, Anita is due for a good night's sleep. Which is when Dominga makes good on her promise...

WOLVERINE VARIANT BY RON LIM

DOMINGA SALVADOR HAD MEANT TO KILL ME. SHE SENT TWO ZOMBIES, ONE ALMOST NEW. THE ZOMBIES WOULD KEEP TRYING UNTIL THEY WERE INCINERATED OR DOMINGA CHANGED HER ORDERS.

DOMINGA HAD GIVEN HER WORD THAT SHE DIDN'T RAISE THE KILLER ZOMBIE, BUT MAYBE HER WORD DIDN'T MEAN ANYTHING. OTHERWISE WHY WOULD SHE MAKE SUCH A DAMNED SERIOUS ATTEMPT TO KILL ME?

DAMMIT!

THE COPS WOULD HOLD IT UNTIL THE LAB BOYS ARRIVED. THEY WOULD DO WHAT COULD BE DONE ON SITE, THEN THE ZOMBIE WOULD BE INCINERATED.

DOMINGA SALVADOR HAD RAISED THE KILLER ZOMBIE AND IT HAD GOTTEN AWAY FROM HER. THE GREAT VOODOO QUEEN HAD SCREWED UP ROYALLY.

THAT, MORE THAN THE DEATHS OR THE POSSIBLE MURDER CHARGE, WOULD PISS HER OFF. SHE COULDN'T AFFORD FOR HER REPUTATION TO BE TRASHED LIKE THAT.

NO ONE HAD EVER ATTACKED ME AT HOME, NOT LIKE THIS. IT SHOULD HAVE BEEN AGAINST THE RULES.

I KNOW, I KNOW, BAD GUYS DON'T HAVE RULES.

IF THESE TWO CAME CLEAN, I COULD SAVE THEM ALL.

MY HANDS WERE CLEANER. THE WATER WASN'T.

SIGMUND WAS SPECIAL...

...THE PENGUIN I OCCASIONALLY SLEPT WITH. I ALMOST TUCKED HIM UNDER MY ARM TO HOLD WHILE I GAVE A STATEMENT. DOLPH PROBABLY WOULDN'T TELL.

THESE ARE THE BIGGEST FREAKING ANGELFISH I'VE EVER SEEN. YOU COULD FRY SOME OF 'EM UP IN A PAN.

LEAVE THE FISH ALONE, ZERBROWSKI.

IF DOLPH WAS UPSET THAT I'D ALMOST CASHED IT IN TONIGHT, HE DIDN'T SHOW IT. BUT THEN DOLPH DIDN'T SHOW MUCH OF ANYTHING, EVER.

THE MOST EMOTION I'D EVER SEEN HIM DISPLAY WAS ABOUT THIS CASE. KILLER ZOMBIE. BUTCHERED CIVILIANS.

YOU'VE ALREADY GOT DOMINGA SALVADOR PISSED AT YOU, ANITA. ISN'T THAT ENOUGH FOR ONE WEEK?

YEAH. I'LL ARRANGE IT. CALL MR. BURKE TOMORROW MORNING AND SET UP A TIME. THEN CALL ME.

WILL DO.

AND WATCH YOUR BACK.

ALWAYS.

FOR ONE LIFETIME. BUT IT'S SOMETHING WE CAN DO WHILE WE WAIT FOR THE WARRANT.

NICE PENGUINS.

STUFFED ANIMALS WERE NOT MEANT TO BE SUBMERGED IN WATER. MAYBE SPOT REMOVER WOULD WORK?

CRISP N' CLEAN, NO MESS IS TOO MUCH. PLEASE LEAVE A MESSAGE AT THE BEEP AND WE'LL GET RIGHT BACK TO YOU.

BEEP!

MY SECRET WAS OUT. ZERBROWSKI WOULD SPREAD IT FAR AND WIDE THAT I COLLECTED TOY PENGUINS. AT LEAST HE WAS CONSISTENT.

IT WAS NICE TO KNOW SOMETHING WAS.

THIS IS ANITA BLAKE, I HAVE AN ACCOUNT. COULD YOU PLEASE SEND SOMEONE AROUND TOMORROW FOR AN EMERGENCY CLEANING? THERE'S BEEN AN... ACCIDENT. THANKS.

I DIDN'T REALLY BELIEVE THAT DOMINGA HAD BACKUP ZOMBIES WAITING TO JUMP ME. BUT SOMEHOW I WAS FEELING PARANOID THIS MORNING. PARANOIA IS JUST ANOTHER WORD FOR LONGEVITY.

MOST PEOPLE FEAR THE DARK IN A VAGUE WAY. THEY FEAR WHAT MIGHT BE OUT THERE.

I RAISE THE DEAD. I'VE SLAIN OVER A DOZEN VAMPIRES. I KNOW WHAT'S OUT THERE IN THE DARK.

AND I AM TERRIFIED OF IT.

RAISING A ZOMBIE FOR THE PURPOSE OF BEING A MURDER WEAPON IS AN AUTOMATIC DEATH SENTENCE. IF WE COULD GET PROOF, THE STATE WOULD KILL DOMINGA SALVADOR FOR ME.

JOHN BURKE, TOO, IF WE COULD PROVE HE HAD KNOWINGLY CAUSED THE ZOMBIE TO GO APE-SHIT.

THE TROUBLE WITH SUPERNATURAL CRIMES IS PROVING THEM IN COURT. MOST JURIES AREN'T UP ON THE LATEST SPELLS AND INCANTATIONS.

I COULD TASTE DAWN ON THE AIR. MAYBE IT WAS ALL THE VAMPIRE HUNTING, BUT I WAS MORE ATTUNED TO THE PASSAGE OF LIGHT AND DARK THAN I HAD BEEN FOUR YEARS AGO.

OF COURSE MY NIGHTMARES WERE A LOT LESS INTERESTING FOUR YEARS AGO. YOU GAIN SOMETHING, YOU LOSE SOMETHING ELSE. IT'S THE WAY LIFE WORKS.

THE STOUFFER CONCOURSE WASN'T TERRIBLY CHEAP BUT IT WOULD FORCE ZOMBIES TO RIDE UP IN ELEVATORS. PEOPLE TENDED TO NOTICE THE SMELL IN AN ELEVATOR.

IT ALSO HAD ROOM SERVICE AT THIS UNGODLY HOUR. I NEEDED COFFEE.

THERE'S SOMETHING ABOUT BEING NAKED THAT MAKES ME FEEL VULNERABLE. I WOULD MUCH RATHER FACE BAD GUYS WITH MY CLOTHES ON.

DOMINGA SALVADOR HAD RAISED A ZOMBIE AND IT HAD ESCAPED HER CONTROL COMPLETELY. SHE WOULD RATHER HAVE INNOCENT PEOPLE SLAUGHTERED THAN ADMIT IT. AND SHE WOULD RATHER KILL ME THAN HAVE ME PROVE IT.

VINDICTIVE BITCH.

SHE HAD TO BE STOPPED. IF THE WARRANT DIDN'T HELP, THEN I'D HAVE TO BE MORE PRACTICAL. SHE'D MADE IT CLEAR THAT IT WAS HER OR ME.

I PREFERRED IT TO BE HER. AND IF NECESSARY, I'D MAKE SURE OF IT.

I WANTED SEVERAL THINGS. DOMINGA OUT OF THE PICTURE, DEAD OR IN JAIL.

TO STAY ALIVE AND NOT BE IN JAIL ON A MURDER CHARGE. TO CATCH THE KILLER ZOMBIE BEFORE IT KILLED AGAIN.

FAT CHANCE OF THAT.

TO FIGURE OUT HOW JOHN BURKE FIT INTO THIS MESS. AND TO KEEP HAROLD GAYNOR FROM FORCING ME TO PERFORM A HUMAN SACRIFICE.

I ALMOST FORGOT THAT ONE.

BY EIGHT THAT MORNING I KNEW MORE ABOUT MR. HAROLD GAYNOR THAT I WANTED TO, NONE OF IT PARTICULARLY HELPFUL.

GAYNOR WAS MOB-CONNECTED, BUT IT COULDN'T BE PROVEN. HE WAS A SELF-MADE MULTI-MILLIONAIRE.

HIS ONLY FAMILY HAD BEEN A MOTHER WHO DIED TEN YEARS AGO. HIS FATHER DIDN'T SEEM TO EXIST. AN ILLEGITIMATE BIRTH? MAYBE.

WHY HAD WANDA LEFT? JEALOUSY? HAD CICELY ARRANGED IT? HAD GAYNOR TIRED OF HER? THE ONLY WAY TO KNOW WAS TO ASK.

IF SHE HATED GAYNOR MORE THAN SHE FEARED HIM, WANDA WOULD TALK TO ME. SHE WOULD BE A FOOL TO TALK TO THE PAPERS, BUT I DIDN'T WANT TO PUBLISH HER SECRETS. I WANTED GAYNOR'S SECRETS, SO I COULD KEEP HIM FROM HURTING ME.

I HAD CALLED AND LEFT A MESSAGE FOR JOHN BURKE AND I WAS ACHINGLY TIRED.

IRVING WOULD JUST HAVE TO WAIT FOR HIS FILE. I HAD UNINTENTIONALLY GIVEN HIM THE INTERVIEW WITH THE MASTER OF THE CITY. SURELY THAT CUT ME A LITTLE SLACK.

I DIDN'T WANT TO HEAR THAT JEAN-CLAUDE WAS CHARMING OR HAD GREAT PLANS FOR THE CITY. HE'D BE VERY CAREFUL WHAT HE TOLD A REPORTER.

BUT I KNEW THE TRUTH. VAMPIRES ARE AS MUCH A MONSTER AS ANY ZOMBIE, MAYBE WORSE.

IF IRVING HADN'T BEEN WITH ME, THE MASTER WOULD HAVE LEFT HIM ALONE. PROBABLY. SO IT WAS MY FAULT. SORT OF.

I KNEW I'D NEVER BE ABLE TO SLEEP UNTIL I HEARD IRVING'S VOICE.

HELLO?

HI, IRVING, IT'S ME.

I HAD A BIT OF EXCITEMENT AT MY APARTMENT LAST NIGHT. I WAS HOPING I COULD DROP THE FILE OFF LATER IN THE DAY.

WHAT SORT OF EXCITEMENT?

THE KIND THAT'S POLICE BUSINESS AND NOT YOURS.

MS. BLAKE, TO WHAT DO I OWE THIS EARLY MORNING PLEASURE?

I THOUGHT YOU'D SAY THAT. YOU JUST GETTING TO BED? I GUESS I CAN LET A HARDWORKING ANIMATOR SLEEP IN A LITTLE.

THANKS, IRVING.

CUT IT OUT, RONNIE. YOU SHOULD STAY AS FAR AWAY FROM THAT...*CREATURE*... AS YOU CAN, ANITA.

I KNOW IT. AGREEING TO MEET HIM SEEMED THE LESSER OF EVILS.

WHAT WERE YOUR CHOICES?

MEETING HIM VOLUNTARILY OR BEING KIDNAPPED AND TAKEN TO MEET HIM.

GREAT CHOICES.

IT HAS TO BE OVER A HUNDRED TODAY.

NO PAIN, NO GAIN.

FOUR MILES IN HELL. LET'S DO IT.

ST. LOUIS IN THE SUMMERTIME. *YIPPEE.*

SLIM HIPS AND MUSCULAR CALVES ARE NOT INCENTIVE ENOUGH FOR THIS KIND OF ABUSE.

BEING ABLE TO OUTRUN THE BAD GUY IS, THOUGH.

I DON'T MEAN TO BE AN ALARMIST, BUT WHY IS THAT MAN JUST STANDING THERE?

HOW LONG'S HE BEEN THERE?

JUST STEPPED AROUND FROM BEHIND THE TREE.

LET'S TURN BACK. IT'S TWO MILES EITHER WAY.

RUN.

UN-UH. I DON'T FEEL LIKE CHASING ANYONE IN THIS HEAT. ALL YA GOTTA BE IS ALIVE, CHICKIE, ANYTHING ELSE IS GRAVY.

WHAT DO YOU WANT?

YOU TO COME FOR A LITTLE RIDE WITH US, THAT'S ALL.

DON'T YOU TALK?

I TALK.

I TALK *REAL* GOOD.

NONE OF THAT, SEYMOUR. NO MESSING AROUND AND WE CAN'T KILL HER--THOSE ARE THE *RULES*.

SHIT, PETE.

YOU CAN HAVE THE BLONDE. NO ONE SAID WE COULDN'T HAVE FUN WITH HER.

PHALLIC POWER, RONNIE. IT ALWAYS GOES TO THE GONADS.

WHAT THE HELL DOES THAT MEAN?

IT MEANS, SEYMOUR, THAT I THINK YOU'RE STUPID AND WHAT BRAINS YOU HAVE ARE IN YOUR BALLS.

THE LAUGHING CORPSE WAS ONE OF THE NEWEST CLUBS IN THE DISTRICT. VAMPIRES ARE SEXY. I'LL ADMIT THAT. BUT *FUNNY?* I DON'T THINK SO.

APPARENTLY, I WAS IN THE MINORITY.

HEY!

SORRY.

YOU CAN'T JUST CUT IN LINE LIKE THAT, MA'AM.

MA'AM?

I DON'T WANT A TICKET. I AM SUPPOSED TO MEET JEAN-CLAUDE HERE. THAT'S IT.

WELL, I DON'T KNOW. HOW DO I KNOW YOU'RE NOT SOME REPORTER?

JUST CALL JEAN-CLAUDE AND TELL HIM ANITA IS HERE, OKAY? IF I'M JUST A NOSY REPORTER, HE'LL DEAL WITH ME.

IF I AM WHO I SAY I AM, HE'LL BE HAPPY THAT YOU CALLED HIM. EITHER WAY YOU CAN'T LOSE.

WILLIE, YOU SEND HER THROUGH?

ANITA, GOOD TO SEE YA.

YOU, TOO, WILLIE.

THE LAUGHING CORPSE

IT'S A SCREAM!

I *WAS* GLAD TO SEE HIM. THAT SURPRISED ME. I'M NOT USUALLY HAPPY TO SEE DEAD MEN.

REALLY?

YEAH.

HOW LONG HAVE YOU BEEN MANAGER HERE?

'BOUT TWO WEEKS.

CONGRATULATIONS.

THANKS TO ME HELPING YOU LAST TIME, I'M IN REAL GOOD WITH THE BOSS.

I'M GLAD JEAN-CLAUDE'S DOING RIGHT BY YOU.

WOULD YOU LIKE A DRINK WHILE YA WAIT?

COULD I HAVE A COKE?

NUTHIN' STRONGER?

NAH.

ERNIE HERE IS THE BEST ROOMMATE I EVER HAD.

HE DOESN'T EAT, DOESN'T TALK MY EAR OFF, DOESN'T BRING CUTE CHICKS HOME AND LOCK ME OUT WHILE THEY HAVE A GOOD TIME.

THOUGH THERE WAS THAT PORK CHOP IN THE FRIDGE THAT WENT BAD. ERNIE SEEMED TO LIKE THAT A LOT.

ENJOY.

AS SOON AS I TOUCHED HIS ARM, I WISHED I HADN'T. IT WAS LIKE TOUCHING WOOD. IT WAS DEAD, NO FEELING OF MOVEMENT, OF LIFE.

WILLIE MCCOY WAS THE ONLY VAMPIRE I HAD EVER KNOWN BEFORE HE DIED. HE HAD BEEN A SMALL-TIME HOOD, AN ERRAND BOY FOR BIGGER FISH.

MAYBE WILLIE THOUGHT BEING A VAMPIRE WOULD MAKE HIM A BIG FISH.

HE'D BEEN WRONG THERE. HE WAS JUST A LITTLE UNDEAD FISH NOW. JEAN-CLAUDE OR SOMEONE LIKE HIM WOULD RUN WILLIE'S 'LIFE' FOR ETERNITY.

POOR WILLIE.

RELEASE HIM.

FLUMP

THANKS.

LADIES AND GENTLEMEN, THE AMAZING ALBERT AND HIS PET ZOMBIE!

CLAP CLAP CLAP CLAP CLAP

ERNIE THINKS IT'S TIME TO GO HOME NOW. YOU'VE BEEN A GREAT AUDIENCE.

CLAP CLAP CLAPCLAP

FOLLOW ALBERT AND OBEY HIS ORDERS UNTIL I TELL YOU OTHER-WISE.

I SPEAK AND ZOMBIES LISTEN. IT DOESN'T EVEN FEEL LIKE MAGIC TO ME.

WHY WOULD I TELL JEAN-CLAUDE?

YOU'RE HIS HUMAN SERVANT, WHETHER YOU LIKE IT OR NOT. WHEN WE SPEAK TO YOU, HE TELLS US WE'RE SPEAKING TO HIM.

YOU KNOW I'M NOT HIS HUMAN SERVANT.

BUT HE WANTS YOU TO BE.

JUST BECAUSE JEAN-CLAUDE WANTS SOMETHING DOESN'T MEAN HE GETS IT.

YOU DON'T KNOW WHAT HE'S LIKE.

I THINK I DO...

HE'S BEEN DIFFERENT SINCE THE OLD MASTER DIED. HE'S A LOT MORE POWERFUL THAN EVEN YOU KNOW.

THIS MUCH I HAD SUSPECTED.

SO WHY SHOULDN'T I TELL HIM YOU'RE AFRAID OF ZOMBIES?

HE'LL USE IT TO PUNISH ME.

YOU MEAN HE'S TORTURING PEOPLE TO CONTROL THEM.

SHIT.

YOU WON'T TELL?

I WON'T TELL. PROMISE.

HIS HAND DIDN'T FEEL WOOD HARD ANYMORE. WHY? I DIDN'T KNOW, AND I BET WILLIE DIDN'T KNOW EITHER. ONE OF THE MANY MYSTERIES OF...DEATH.

THANKS.

I THOUGHT YOU SAID THAT JEAN-CLAUDE WAS THE KINDEST MASTER YOU'VE EVER HAD?

HE IS.

IF BEING TORMENTED BY YOUR DARKEST FEAR WAS THE KINDEST, HOW MUCH WORSE HAD NIKOLAOS BEEN?

THANKS FOR YOUR HELP WITH THE ZOMBIE.

YOU WERE BRAVE, YOU KNOW.

I CAN'T AFFORD TO BE ANYTHING ELSE.

WILLIE WAS MOVING UP IN THE RANKS. A SIGN OF WEAKNESS COULD STOP THAT RISE. OR WORSE.

I WENT TO NEW YORK, TOUGH CITY. A GANG JUMPED ME, BUT I PUT THE BITE ON THEM.

I DIDN'T GET IT. IT WAS NOT FUNNY.

HE WAS USING MIND TRICKS. I'D SEEN VAMPIRES SEDUCE, THREATEN, TERRIFY, ALL BY CONCENTRATING. BUT I HAD NEVER SEEN THEM CAUSE LAUGHTER.

MASS MIND CONTROL WAS ONE OF THE TOP SCARY THINGS THAT MOST PEOPLE DON'T KNOW VAMPIRES CAN DO. I KNEW, AND I DIDN'T LIKE IT.

HE WAS THE FRESH DEAD, AND EVEN BEFORE JEAN-CLAUDE'S MARKS, THE COMIC COULDN'T HAVE TOUCHED ME. BEING AN ANIMATOR GAVE ME PARTIAL IMMUNITY TO VAMPIRES.

I HAD CALLED CHARLES EARLIER TO ESCORT ME TO FIND WANDA, HAROLD GAYNOR'S FORMER GIRLFRIEND. WHERE WAS HE?

AND WHEN WOULD JEAN-CLAUDE BE READY TO SEE ME? TRUST HIM TO BROWBEAT ME INTO A MEETING AND THEN MAKE ME WAIT.

...I RUN A VERY GOOD, CLEAN KITCHEN.

WHAT ARE YOU, THE DAMN HEALTH DEPARTMENT?

DO NOT TOUCH ME.

I SAID, I RUN A CLEAN KITCHEN.

YOU CAN'T HAVE ZOMBIES NEAR THE FOOD PREPARATION. IT'S ILLEGAL. THE HEALTH CODES FORBID CORPSES NEAR FOOD.

MY ASSISTANT IS A VAMPIRE. HE'S DEAD.

ZOMBIES ROT AND CARRY DISEASE LIKE ANY DEAD BODY, MR. KIM. JUST BECAUSE THEY MOVE AROUND DOESN'T MEAN THEY AREN'T A REPOSITORY FOR DISEASE.

EITHER KEEP THE ZOMBIES AWAY FROM THE KITCHEN OR WE WILL CLOSE YOU DOWN. DO YOU UNDERSTAND THAT?

AND YOU'D HAVE TO EXPLAIN TO THE OWNER WHY HIS BUSINESS WAS NOT MAKING MONEY.

I...I UNDERSTAND. IT WILL BE TAKEN CARE OF.

GOOD.

I GOT YOUR MESSAGE. WHAT'S GOING ON?

I NEED AN ESCORT TO THE TENDERLOIN.

WHY IN THE WORLD DO YOU WANT TO GO DOWN THERE?

I NEED TO FIND SOMEONE WHO WORKS DOWN THERE.

WHO?

A PROSTITUTE.

CAROLINE IS NOT GOING TO LIKE THIS.

DON'T TELL HER.

YOU KNOW CAROLINE AND I DON'T LIE TO EACH OTHER, ABOUT ANYTHING.

CAROLINE THOUGHT THAT OUR JOB WAS GROSS. BEHEADING CHICKENS, RAISING ZOMBIES, HOW UNCOUTH.

JUST TELL HER THAT YOU HAD EXTRA ANIMATOR BUSINESS.

WHY DO YOU NEED TO FIND THIS PROSTITUTE?

I JUST NEED SOMEONE TO LOOK MENACING. I DON'T WANT TO HAVE TO SHOOT SOME POOR SLOB BECAUSE HE MADE A PASS AT ME. OKAY?

I'LL COME. I'M FLATTERED.

TRUTH WAS, MANNY WAS MORE DANGEROUS AND MUCH BETTER BACKUP. BUT MANNY DIDN'T LOOK DANGEROUS. I NEEDED A GOOD BLUFF TONIGHT, NOT FIREPOWER.

WHAT YA WANT?

IS JEAN-CLAUDE READY TO SEE ME OR NOT?

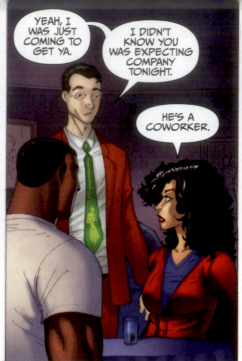

YEAH, I WAS JUST COMING TO GET YA.

I DIDN'T KNOW YOU WAS EXPECTING COMPANY TONIGHT.

HE'S A COWORKER.

A ZOMBIE RAISER?

YES.

SURE, YA GOT ZOMBIE WORK AFTER YOU SEE JEAN-CLAUDE?

YEAH.

I'LL BE AS QUICK AS I CAN.

ALL RIGHT, BUT I NEED TO GET HOME SOON.

HE WAS ON A SHORT LEASH. HIS OWN FAULT, BUT IT SEEMED TO BOTHER ME MORE THAN IT BOTHERED CHARLES. MAYBE IT WAS ONE OF THE REASONS I'M NOT MARRIED.

I'M NOT BIG ON COMPROMISE.

NO, IT ISN'T. AND STOP CALLING ME *MA PETITE.*

ANGER REPLACED FEAR IN A QUICK, WARM RUSH. I LIKED ANGER. IT MADE ME BRAVE, AND STUPID.

SCREW YOU.

I HAVE ALREADY OFFERED YOU THAT.

DAMN YOU, JEAN-CLAUDE.

WE NEED TO TALK, *MA PETITE.*

THEN TALK. I HAVEN'T GOT ALL NIGHT.

PLEASE, BE SEATED.

I DON'T HAVE THAT KIND OF TIME.

I THOUGHT WE HAD AGREED TO TALK THIS OUT, *MA PETITE.*

WE AGREED TO MEET AT ELEVEN. YOU'RE THE ONE WHO WASTED AN HOUR, NOT ME.

VERY WELL. I WILL GIVE YOU A...CONDENSED VERSION.

FINE WITH ME.

TO SURVIVE WITH NIKOLAOS ALIVE, I HAD TO HIDE MY POWERS. I DID IT TOO WELL.

THERE ARE THOSE WHO THINK I AM NOT POWERFUL ENOUGH TO BE THE MASTER OF ALL. THEY ARE CHALLENGING ME. ONE OF THE THINGS THEY ARE USING AGAINST ME IS YOU.

HOW?

YOUR DISOBEDIENCE. I CANNOT EVEN CONTROL MY OWN HUMAN SERVANT. HOW CAN I POSSIBLY CONTROL ALL THE VAMPIRES IN THE CITY AND SURROUNDING AREAS?

WHAT DO YOU WANT FROM ME?

I WANT YOU TO BE MY HUMAN SERVANT.

NOT IN THIS LIFETIME, JEAN-CLAUDE. I WOULD RATHER DIE.

I CAN FORCE THE THIRD MARK ON YOU, ANITA.

IF YOU FORCE THIS ISSUE, I WILL KILL YOU.

MASTER VAMPIRES CAN SMELL THE TRUTH.

YOU MEAN THAT.

YES.

I DO NOT UNDERSTAND YOU, MA PETITE.

I KNOW.

COULD YOU PRETEND TO BE MY SERVANT?

WHAT DOES PRETENDING MEAN?

YOU COME TO A FEW MEETINGS. YOU STAND AT MY SIDE WITH YOUR GUNS AND YOUR REPUTATION.

A KIND GOD HAD MADE CHARLES LOOK BIG AND BAD, BECAUSE INSIDE HE WAS ALL MARSHMALLOW. IF I'D HAD CHARLES'S NATURAL SIZE AND STRENGTH, I'D HAVE BEEN A GUARANTEED BADASS.

IT WAS SORT OF SAD AND UNFAIR.

WHAT'S WRONG?

MM-HMM.

I CALLED CAROLINE. THE BABYSITTER'S SICK, AND CAROLINE'S BEEN CALLED IN TO THE HOSPITAL. SOMEONE HAS TO STAY WITH SAM WHILE SHE GOES TO WORK.

CAN GOING DOWN TO THE TENDERLOIN WAIT UNTIL TOMORROW?

NO.

YOU'RE NOT GOING TO GO DOWN THERE ALONE.

ARE YOU?

I CAN'T WAIT, CHARLES.

YOU CAN'T GO DOWN THERE ALONE AT NIGHT, ANITA.

SO WHY KEEP ME AROUND?

PERHAPS IF NIKOLAOS HAD HAD SUCH A MIRROR, SHE WOULD NOT HAVE BEEN SUCH A MONSTER.

THE TENDERLOIN WAS ORIGINALLY THE RED LIGHT DISTRICT ON THE RIVERFRONT IN THE 1800'S. BUT THE TENDERLOIN, LIKE SO MUCH OF ST. LOUIS, MOVED UPTOWN.

PIMPS BEWARE. I WAS BRINGING THE MASTER OF THE CITY AS BACKUP. IT WAS LIKE CARRYING A THERMONUCLEAR DEVICE TO KILL ANTS.

ARE YOU IN THERE, JEAN-CLAUDE?

HE MIGHT BE RIGHT. IT MADE HIS CHOICE OF ME AS HUMAN SERVANT ALMOST NOBLE. OH, HELL, I WOULD NOT START FEELING SORRY FOR THE FREAKING MASTER OF THE CITY.

NOT NOW. NOT EVER.

HE SAID NOTHING. HIS EYES GLITTERING IN THE NEON SIGNS LIKE DARK GLASS.

YOU CAN PLAY HUMAN, JEAN-CLAUDE, BETTER THAN ALMOST ANY VAMPIRE I'VE EVER MET. WHAT'S ALL THIS SUPERNATURAL CRAP?

CRAP?

YEAH, WHY ARE YOU GOING ALL SPOOKY ON ME?

SPOOKY?

YOU HAVEN'T FED YET TONIGHT, HAVE YOU?

YOU ARE THE VAMPIRE EXPERT. CAN YOU NOT TELL?

MANY PEOPLE CONFUSE THE TWO.

YOU KNOW I CAN NEVER TELL WITH YOU.

A COMPLIMENT TO MY POWERS, I'M SURE.

I DID NOT BRING YOU DOWN HERE TO *HUNT*.

WOULD YOU FORBID ME TO HUNT TONIGHT?

I HAVE NO PERSONAL STAKE IN THESE PEOPLE, JEAN-CLAUDE, BUT THEY *ARE* PEOPLE. GOOD, BAD, OR INDIFFERENT, THEY ARE ALIVE, AND NO ONE HAS THE RIGHT TO JUST ARBITRARILY SNUFF THEM OUT.

SO IT IS THE SANCTITY OF LIFE YOU CLING TO?

THAT AND THE FACT THAT EVERY HUMAN BEING IS SPECIAL. EVERY DEATH IS A LOSS OF SOMETHING PRECIOUS AND IRREPLACEABLE.

YOU HAVE KILLED BEFORE, ANITA. YOU HAVE DESTROYED THAT WHICH IS IRREPLACEABLE.

I'M IRREPLACEABLE, TOO.

NO ONE HAS THE RIGHT TO KILL ME, EITHER.

HE SAT UP IN ONE LIQUID MOTION, AND REALITY SEEMED TO COLLECT AROUND HIM.

HE SUDDENLY LOOKED MUCH MORE HUMAN.

JESUS.

WHAT IS WRONG, *MA PETITE?*

IF I ASKED HOW HE DID IT, HE'D JUST SMILE.

WHAT DID YOU DO TO HER?

I'LL DO YOU FOR FREE.

NOTHING.

NOTHING, AND SHE OFFERS TO DO YOU FOR FREE?

BE STILL.

DON'T TELL ME TO SHUT UP.

THE WOMAN'S HANDS DROPPED TO HER SIDES. HE HADN'T BEEN TALKING TO ME.

I WAITED FOR HER TO MOVE. SOMETHING.

THEN SHE CAME BACK TO LIFE AND CALLED TO A NEW CUSTOMER AS IF WE'D NEVER EXISTED.

DAMMIT, WHAT DID YOU DO TO HER?

I TOLD YOU, MA PETITE, NOTHING.

DON'T CALL ME THAT.

I SAW HER, JEAN-CLAUDE. DON'T LIE TO ME.

WILL YOU JUST TELL ME--

WHAT WAS YOUR FAULT?

IT WAS CARELESS OF ME, *MA*...ANITA. MY FAULT ENTIRELY.

MY...POWERS ARE GREATER WHEN MY HUMAN SERVANT IS WITH ME.

WITH YOU BESIDE ME, THEY ARE ENHANCED.

WAIT, YOU MEAN LIKE A WITCH'S FAMILIAR?

YES, VERY CLOSE TO THAT.

SO YOUR ABILITY TO *BESPELL* PEOPLE WITH YOUR EYES IS STRONGER WHEN I'M WITH YOU. STRONG ENOUGH THAT WITHOUT TRYING, YOU BESPELLED THAT PROSTITUTE.

YES.

NO, I DON'T BELIEVE YOU.

BELIEVE WHAT YOU LIKE, *MA PETITE.* IT IS THE TRUTH.

I DIDN'T *WANT* TO BELIEVE IT. BECAUSE IF IT WERE TRUE, I WAS IN FACT HIS HUMAN SERVANT. NOT IN MY ACTIONS BUT BY MY VERY PRESENCE.

SHIT.

YOU COULD SAY THAT.

NO, I CAN'T DEAL WITH THIS RIGHT NOW. YOU KEEP WHATEVER POWERS WE HAVE BETWEEN US IN CHECK, OKAY?

I WILL TRY.

DON'T *TRY,* DAMMIT, *DO IT.*

OF COURSE, *MA PETITE.*

IF YOU CALL ME THAT ONE MORE TIME, I'M GOING TO HIT YOU.

I HATE IT WHEN PEOPLE FIND MY THREATS AMUSING. I WANTED TO HURT HIM BECAUSE HE SCARED ME.

WHAT IS IT, ANITA?

DON'T PUSH ME INTO A CORNER, JEAN-CLAUDE. YOU DON'T WANT TO TAKE AWAY ALL MY OPTIONS.

I DON'T KNOW WHAT YOU MEAN.

IF IT COMES DOWN TO YOU OR ME, I'M GOING TO PICK ME. YOU REMEMBER THAT.

I BELIEVE YOU WOULD. BUT REMEMBER, *MA...*ANITA, IF YOU HURT ME, IT HURTS YOU. I COULD SURVIVE THE STRAIN OF YOUR DEATH.

THE QUESTION, *MA BELLOTE*, IS COULD YOU SURVIVE MINE?

DAMN YOU, JEAN-CLAUDE, *DAMN YOU.*

A NEW FRENCH PHRASE I DIDN'T WANT TO KNOW.

THAT, DEAR ANITA, WAS DONE LONG BEFORE YOU MET ME.

WHAT DOES THAT MEAN?

WHY, ANITA, YOUR OWN CATHOLIC CHURCH HAS DECLARED ALL VAMPIRES AS SUICIDES. WE ARE AUTOMATICALLY DAMNED.

I'M EPISCOPALIAN NOW, BUT THAT ISN'T WHAT YOU MEANT.

THERE WAS NOBODY ON THIS STREET AS DANGEROUS AS JEAN-CLAUDE. I HAD BROUGHT HIM DOWN HERE TO PROTECT ME. THAT WAS LAUGHABLE. RIDICULOUS.

OBSCENE.

COULD WE TALK?

SURE, YOU GOT A ROOM?

WASN'T SHE SUPPOSED TO HAVE THE ROOM?

NO.

SHE JUST LOOKED AT ME LIKE I WAS SUPPOSED TO DO SOMETHING.

WE JUST WANT TO TALK TO YOU FOR AN HOUR, OR TWO. WE'LL PAY WHATEVER THE GOING RATE IS.

THREE-FIFTY.

JESUS, THAT'S A LITTLE STEEP.

SUPPLY AND DEMAND. YOU CAN'T GET A TASTE OF WHAT I HAVE ANYWHERE ELSE.

OKAY, YOU GOT A DEAL.

IT WAS A BUSINESS EXPENSE. COMPUTER PAPER, INK PENS, ONE PROSTITUTE, MANILA FOLDERS. SEE, IT FIT RIGHT IN.

BERT WAS GOING TO LOVE THIS ONE.

THERE ARE NO ELEVATORS IN MY APARTMENT BUILDING. THE ONLY CONSOLATION WAS THAT I GOT TO WATCH JEAN-CLAUDE CLIMB TWO FLIGHT OF STAIRS. SO SUE ME.

HE HAD A VERY NICE BACKSIDE FOR A VAMPIRE. BUT I WAS CAREFUL HE DIDN'T CATCH ME LOOKING.

WHAT'S WRONG?

I HAVE NEVER BEEN TO YOUR APARTMENT.

SO?

THE GREAT VAMPIRE EXPERT... COME, ANITA.

YOU HAVE MY PERMISSION TO ENTER MY HOME.

I AM HONORED.

WOULD YOU LIKE SOMETHING TO DRINK?

RED WINE, IF YOU HAVE IT.

SORRY, NOTHING ALCOHOLIC. COFFEE, NON-DIET SOFT DRINKS, AND WATER, THAT'S ABOUT IT.

SOFT DRINK.

YOU WANT A GLASS?

NO.

I DON'T NEED A GLASS, EITHER.

DON'T GET CUTE.

TOO LATE.

SHIT, HE'S A VAMPIRE.

YOU DIDN'T KNOW?

I COULD ALWAYS TELL. DEAD WAS DEAD TO ME, NO MATTER HOW PRETTY THE CORPSE.

NO, I'M NOT COFFIN-BAIT.

WHAT'S COFFIN-BAIT?

A WHORE THAT DOES VAMPIRES.

HOW QUAINT.

HE WON'T TOUCH YOU.

HOW TERRIFYING TO GO AWAY WITH STRANGERS AND NOT KNOW IF THEY WILL HURT YOU OR NOT. DESPERATION, OR A DEATH WISH.

SO YOU AND I ARE GOING TO DO IT?

NO.

NO, I SAID I JUST WANTED TO TALK. I MEANT IT.

YOU WANT ME TO TALK ABOUT DOING IT WITH OTHER PEOPLE, WHILE YOU DO IT WITH HIM?

LOOK, WANDA, WE ARE JUST GOING TO TALK. THAT'S IT. NOBODY IS GOING TO DO ANYTHING TO ANYBODY.

OKAY?

IT'S YOUR MONEY. WE CAN DO WHATEVER YOU WANT.

SHE WOULD DO ANYTHING I WANTED. ANYTHING? IT WAS TOO AWFUL, THAT A HUMAN BEING WOULD SAY "ANYTHING" AND MEAN IT.

OF COURSE, SHE DREW THE LINE AT VAMPIRES. EVEN WHORES HAVE STANDARDS.

I HEARD YOU WERE HAROLD GAYNOR'S MISTRESS A WHILE BACK.

I DON'T KNOW THE NAME.

COME ON, WANDA, I KNOW YOU WERE GAYNOR'S SWEETIE. ADMIT YOU KNOW HIM, AND WE'LL WORK FROM THERE.

NO. I'LL DO YOU. I'LL LET THE VAMP WATCH. I'LL TALK DIRTY TO YOU BOTH.

BUT I DON'T KNOW ANYBODY NAMED GAYNOR.

I'M NOT A REPORTER. GAYNOR WILL NEVER KNOW YOU TALKED TO ME UNLESS YOU TELL HIM.

TALK TO ME, WANDA.

WHO THE HELL *ARE* YOU? YOU'RE NOT COPS. YOU'RE NOT REPORTERS. SOCIAL WORKERS DON'T CARRY GUNS. WHO ARE YOU?

TROUBLE, *MA PETITE?*

SHE'S BEING STUBBORN.

HE'LL KILL ME.

HE'LL NEVER KNOW.

AND, MY SWEET COQUETTE, HE IS NOT HERE WITH YOU TONIGHT.

WE ARE.

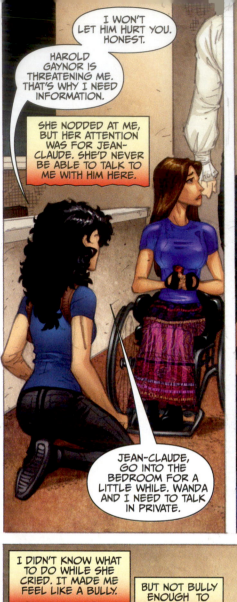

I WON'T LET HIM HURT YOU. HONEST.

HAROLD GAYNOR IS THREATENING ME. THAT'S WHY I NEED INFORMATION.

SHE NODDED AT ME, BUT HER ATTENTION WAS FOR JEAN-CLAUDE. SHE'D NEVER BE ABLE TO TALK TO ME WITH HIM HERE.

JEAN-CLAUDE, GO INTO THE BEDROOM FOR A LITTLE WHILE. WANDA AND I NEED TO TALK IN PRIVATE.

YOUR BEDROOM.

MY PLEASURE, MA PETITE.

YOU REALLY AREN'T GOING TO LET HIM HURT ME, ARE YOU?

NO, I'M NOT.

I DIDN'T KNOW WHAT TO DO WHILE SHE CRIED. IT MADE ME FEEL LIKE A BULLY.

BUT NOT BULLY ENOUGH TO STOP.

CAN WE TALK NOW?

OKAY.

YOU KNOW HAROLD GAYNOR, RIGHT?

IF HE FINDS OUT, HE WILL KILL ME. MAYBE I DON'T WANT TO BE COFFIN-BAIT BUT I SURE AS HELL DON'T WANT TO DIE EITHER.

NO ONE DOES. TALK TO ME, PLEASE.

TELL ME ABOUT HIM.

OKAY, I KNOW HAROLD.

HAS HE SENT BRUNO OR TOMMY AFTER YOU YET?

TOMMY CAME FOR A PERSONAL MEETING.

WHAT HAPPENED?

I DREW A GUN ON HIM.

THAT GUN?

YES.

WHAT DID YOU DO TO MAKE HAROLD MAD?

I REFUSED TO DO SOMETHING FOR HIM.

IT DOESN'T MATTER.

WHAT?

IT CAN'T HAVE BEEN SEX. YOU AREN'T CRIPPLED.

HE DOESN'T TOUCH ANYONE WHO'S WHOLE.

HOW DID YOU MEET HIM?

I WAS IN COLLEGE AT WASH U. GAYNOR WAS DONATING MONEY FOR SOMETHING.

AND HE ASKED YOU OUT?

YEAH.

WHAT HAPPENED?

WE WERE BOTH IN WHEEL-CHAIRS. HE WAS RICH. IT WAS GREAT.

WHEN DID IT STOP BEING GREAT?

I MOVED IN WITH HIM AND DROPPED OUT OF SCHOOL. LIVING OFF HIM WAS...EASIER THAN COLLEGE. IT WAS EASIER THAN ANYTHING.

HE COULDN'T GET ENOUGH OF ME.

HE STARTED WANTING VARIETY IN THE BEDROOM. SEE, HIS LEGS ARE CRIPPLED BUT HE CAN STILL FEEL.

I CAN'T FEEL.

HE LIKED TO DO THINGS TO MY LEGS BUT I COULDN'T FEEL IT. AT FIRST I THOUGHT THAT WAS OKAY, BUT...HE GOT REALLY SICK.

HE CUT ME UP. I COULDN'T FEEL IT BUT THAT'S NOT THE POINT, IS IT?

SHE WAS CRYING AGAIN, AND I DID THE ONLY THING I COULD THINK OF...

...OFFER HER A HAND TO HOLD.

--HE CAN'T HURT YOU ANYMORE.

IT'S ALRIGHT--

EVERYONE HURTS YOU. *YOU* WERE GOING TO HURT ME.

IT WAS A LITTLE LATE TO EXPLAIN GOOD COP, BAD COP TO HER. SHE WOULDN'T HAVE BELIEVED IT ANYWAY.

TELL ME ABOUT GAYNOR.

HE REPLACED ME WITH A DEAF GIRL.

CICELY.

YOU'VE MET HER?

BRIEFLY.

CICELY IS ONE SICK CHICKIE.

SHE LIKES TORTURING PEOPLE...IT GETS HER OFF.

HAROLD SLEPT WITH BOTH OF US AT THE SAME TIME, SOMETIMES. AT THE END IT WAS ALWAYS A THREESOME.

IT GOT REAL ROUGH.

CICELY LIKES KNIVES.

SHE'S REAL GOOD AT SKINNING THINGS.

GAYNOR WOULD KILL ME JUST FOR TELLING YOU HIS BEDROOM SECRETS.

DO YOU KNOW ANY BUSINESS SECRETS?

NO, I SWEAR. HE WAS ALWAYS VERY CAREFUL TO KEEP ME OUT OF THAT.

I THOUGHT AT FIRST IT WAS SO IF THE POLICE CAME, I WOULDN'T BE ARRESTED.

LATER, I REALIZED IT WAS BECAUSE HE KNEW I WOULD BE REPLACED.

HE DIDN'T WANT ME TO KNOW ANYTHING THAT COULD HURT HIM AFTER HE THREW ME AWAY.

GAYNOR HAD DONE WORSE THAN KILL HER. HE'D LEFT HER ALIVE--ALIVE AND AS CRIPPLED INSIDE AS OUT.

I CAN'T TELL YOU ANYTHING BUT BEDROOM TALK. IT WON'T HELP YOU HURT HIM THOUGH.

WHAT DO YOU MEAN?

IS THERE ANY BEDROOM TALK THAT ISN'T ABOUT SEX?

PERSONAL SECRETS BUT NOT SEX. YOU WERE HIS SWEETIE FOR TWO YEARS. HE MUST HAVE TALKED ABOUT SOMETHING OTHER THAN SEX.

I...I GUESS HE TALKED ABOUT HIS FAMILY. HE WAS ILLEGITIMATE. HE WAS OBSESSED WITH HIS REAL FATHER'S FAMILY.

HE KNEW WHO THEY WERE?

THEY WERE RICH, OLD MONEY. HIS MOTHER WAS A HOOKER WHO TURNED INTO A MISTRESS.

WHEN SHE GOT PREGNANT, THEY THREW HER OUT.

WHAT FAMILY?

HE NEVER SAID. I THINK HE THOUGHT I'D BLACK-MAIL THEM OR GO TO THEM WITH HIS DIRTY LITTLE SECRETS.

HE DESPERATELY WANTS THEM TO REGRET NOT WELCOMING HIM INTO THE FAMILY. I THINK HE ONLY MADE HIS MONEY SO HE COULD BE AS RICH AS THEM.

IF HE NEVER GAVE YOU A NAME, HOW DO YOU KNOW HE WASN'T LYING?

YOU WOULDN'T ASK THAT IF YOU COULD HEAR HIM. HE HATES THEM AND HE WANTS HIS BIRTHRIGHT. THEIR MONEY IS HIS BIRTHRIGHT.

LIKE GAYNOR DID TO HIS WOMEN. FREUD IS SO OFTEN AT WORK IN OUR LIVES.

HOW DOES HE PLAN TO GET THEIR MONEY?

NO, HIS FATHER'S FAMILY WERE RIVER PIRATES. THEY SAILED THE MISSISSIPPI AND ROBBED PEOPLE.

GAYNOR WAS PROUD OF THAT BUT ANGRY ABOUT IT.

HAROLD HAD FOUND WHERE SOME OF HIS ANCESTORS WERE BURIED. HE TALKED ABOUT BURIED TREASURE, CAN YOU BELIEVE IT?

WHERE DID THEY GET OFF BEING SO HIGH AND MIGHTY TO HIM WHEN THE WHOLE BUNCH OF THEM WERE DESCENDED FROM THIEVES AND WHORES?

IN THE GRAVES?

IS THERE ANY PLACE...

I WAS GOING TO OFFER HER A TRIP SOMEWHERE, ANYWHERE, ELSE.

YOU ARE A SOCIAL WORKER TYPE AFTER ALL. YOU WANT TO SAVE ME, DON'T YOU?

IS IT TERRIBLY NAIVE TO OFFER YOU A TICKET HOME OR SOMEWHERE?

TERRIBLY. AND WHY SHOULD YOU WANT TO HELP ME? YOU'RE NOT A MAN. YOU DON'T LIKE WOMEN. WHY SHOULD YOU OFFER TO SEND ME HOME?

STUPIDITY.

IT'S NOT STUPID. BUT IT WOULDN'T DO ANY GOOD.

I'M A WHORE. HERE AT LEAST I KNOW THE TOWN, THE PEOPLE. I HAVE REGULARS.

I GET BY.

WITH A LITTLE HELP FROM YOUR FRIENDS.

WHORES DON'T HAVE FRIENDS.

YOU DON'T HAVE TO BE A WHORE. GAYNOR MADE YOU A WHORE BUT YOU DON'T HAVE TO STAY ONE.

JUST CALL A TAXI, OKAY? I DON'T WANT TO TALK ANYMORE.

I COULDN'T CARRY HER DOWNSTAIRS, SO JEAN-CLAUDE HAD TO. WANDA WASN'T HAPPY WITH IT, BUT AS WITH SO MUCH IN HER LIFE, SHE HAD NO CHOICE.

WHAT COULD I DO? I CALLED A TAXI.

I MUST LEAVE YOU NOW, MA PETITE. IT HAS BEEN VERY EDUCATIONAL BUT TIME GROWS SHORT.

YOU'RE GOING TO GO FEED, AREN'T YOU?

DOES IT SHOW?

A LITTLE.

I SHOULD CALL YOU MA VERITÉ, ANITA. YOU ALWAYS TELL ME THE TRUTH ABOUT MYSELF.

IS THAT WHAT VERITÉ MEANS? TRUTH?

YES.

SHIT, SHIT, SHIT, DOUBLE SHIT. THIS WAS NOT THE WAY I WANTED TO SPEND MY SATURDAY MORNING.

BUT WE WERE GETTING OUR WARRANT. YIPPEE. THE TROUBLE WAS I WASN'T *REALLY* A VOODOO EXPERT. I DIDN'T KNOW WHAT TO LOOK FOR.

MAYBE I SHOULD ASK MANNY TO COME ALONG. NO, NO, I DIDN'T WANT HIM NEAR DOMINGA IN CASE SHE DECIDED TO CUT A DEAL AND GIVE HIM TO THE POLICE.

THERE IS NO STATUTE OF LIMITATIONS ON HUMAN SACRIFICE. IT'D BE DOMINGA'S STYLE TO TRADE MY FRIEND FOR HER LIFE.

WHY HADN'T I NOTICED THE NEW MESSAGE LAST NIGHT?

ANITA BLAKE, THIS IS JOHN BURKE. I GOT YOUR MESSAGE. CALL ME ANYTIME AT 314-555-2684. I'M EAGER TO HEAR OF WHAT YOU HAVE.

GREAT, A MURDER SCENE, A TRIP TO THE MORGUE, AND A VISIT TO VOODOO LAND, ALL IN ONE DAY. IT WAS GOING TO BE A BUSY AND UNPLEASANT DAY, LIKE LAST NIGHT AND THE NIGHT BEFORE.

SHIT, I WAS ON A ROLL.

MERLIONI PALED, I'D GOTTEN MY COLOR BACK. DON'T THINK ABOUT WHAT YOU'RE TOUCHING AT THE SAME TIME YOU'RE TRYING TO SEE ALL OF IT.

CLUES, WERE THERE ANY DAMN CLUES IN THIS PLACE?

ARE YOU ALRIGHT, MERLIONI? I WOULDN'T WANT TO CONTINUE IF IT'S UPSETTING YOU.

YOU AIN'T SEEN IT ALL, GIRLIE. I HAVE.

HE WAS GREEN AROUND THE EDGES, SO I PUSHED HIM.

AND ME.

BUT HAVE YOU TOUCHED IT ALL?

YOU WON'T WANT TO TOUCH IT ALL.

THAT MUST HAVE HURT LIKE A SON OF A BITCH.

YOU THINK HE WAS ALIVE WHEN THE LEG WAS PULLED OFF?

I REALLY WASN'T A HUNDRED PERCENT SURE. OH, WELL.

OH, YEAH.

BUT IT MADE MERLIONI GO PALER. HE'D FAINT FIRST.

BUT HE RECOVERED AND UPPED THE ANTE.

CATCH.

MY STOMACH ROILED.

JESUS, MERLIONI, THAT ISN'T FUNNY.

NO, BUT THE LOOK ON YOUR FACE IS.

DON'T THROW IT MERLIONI, NO TEASING.

I DIDN'T EXPECT HIM TO DO IT. THE GAME HAD GONE TOO FAR.

ENOUGH. WHILE YOU TWO ARE PLAYING GROSS-OUT, CAN YOU TELL ME SOMETHING USEFUL?

SURE. THE ZOMBIE CAME IN THROUGH THE SLIDING GLASS DOOR LIKE LAST TIME. IT CHASED THE MAN OR WOMAN BACK IN HERE AND GOT THEM BOTH.

MERLIONI WAS HOLDING SOMETHING NEW UP. IT FROZE ME IN PLACE.

IT WAS A BABY BLANKET. HE HELD IT UP BY THE ONE CLEAN CORNER.

YOU BASTARD.

YOU REFERRING TO ME, BITCH?

DAGO BASTARD.

WE HAD TO KEEP PRETENDING THAT THIS WAS ALRIGHT, THAT THIS WAS DOABLE.

IT WAS OBSCENE. IF THE BET HADN'T HELD ME I'D HAVE RUN SCREAMING FROM THE ROOM.

I TOOK THE BLANKET BECAUSE OF THE BET. I FELT LIKE I'D NEVER WANT TO EAT AGAIN, BUT I'D WIN THIS BET.

HOW OLD?

FAMILY PORTRAIT OUT FRONT, I'D GUESS THREE OR FOUR MONTHS.

IF THEY WOULDN'T MAKE ME LOOK, I'D TAKE THEM ALL TO TONY'S. JUST PLEASE, DON'T MAKE ME LOOK.

BUT I HAD TO, IT WAS MY JOB. MIGHT AS WELL SEE IT AND WIN, AS RUN AND LOSE.

MY STOMACH CONTRACTED, I COUGHED AND ALMOST LOST IT.

I DIDN'T, I HELD ON.

THREE, MAYBE FOUR. ABOUT THE SAME AGE AS BENJAMIN REYNOLDS. WAS THAT COINCIDENCE? HAD TO BE. ZOMBIES WEREN'T THAT CHOOSY.

THAT DOLL HAD TO BELONG TO A DIFFERENT CHILD. THE CHILD WHOSE HAND...

OH, GOD.

I WILL DO MY JOB. I WILL DO MY JOB..

I'M BREAST-FEEDING THE BABY, MAYBE, WHEN I HEAR A LOUD NOISE. HUSBAND GOES TO CHECK.

NOISE WAKES THE LITTLE GIRL, SHE COMES OUT OF HER ROOM TO SEE WHAT'S THE MATTER.

HUSBAND SEES THE MONSTER, GRABS THE CHILD, RUNS FOR THE BEDROOM. THE ZOMBIE TAKES THEM ALL HERE.

KILLS THEM ALL HERE.

MY VOICE SOUNDED DISTANT, CLINICAL. BULLY FOR ME.

INSIDE I FELT HOLLOW AS IF PART OF ME WASN'T THERE ANYMORE.

DID YOU SEE THE RING, MERLIONI?

CATCH.

I HAD TO DO SOMETHING TO MAKE IT LESS TERRIBLE.

IT'S CALLED "GALLOWS HUMOR" FOR REASON.

JESUS!

I WOULDN'T REALLY HAVE THROWN THE HAND. I WOULDN'T.

IT FELT HEAVY, AS IF THE FINGERS SHOULD CURL AROUND MINE AND ASK ME TO TAKE IT FOR A WALK.

THE ROOM WAS HOT AND SPINNING EVER SO SLIGHTLY.

DID I WIN THE BET?

ANITA BLAKE, TOUGH CHICK. ONE NIGHT OF DELECTABLE FEASTING AT TONY'S ON MERLIONI'S TAB.

I HEAR THEY MAKE GREAT SPAGHETTI.

THE MENTION OF FOOD WAS TOO MUCH.

BATHROOM, WHERE?

DOWN THE HALL, THIRD DOOR ON THE LEFT.

MERLIONI CAME OUT AS I WENT IN. HE WAS PALE, I WAS GREEN, BUT I'D WON THE BET.

IN THAT MOMENT I HATED MY JOB.

I KNELT WITH MY FOREHEAD AGAINST THE COOL LINOLEUM OF THE FLOOR. I WAS FEELING BETTER. LUCKY I HADN'T TAKEN TIME TO EAT BREAKFAST.

TAP TAP

WHAT?

IT'S DOLPH. CAN I COME IN?

AT LEAST I HADN'T THROWN UP ON THE CORPSES. THAT WAS SOMETHING.

SURE.

SERGEANT DOLPH STORR WAS IN CHARGE OF THE REGIONAL PRETERNATURAL INVESTIGATION TEAM, AND I WAS SUPPOSED TO BE HELPING THEM SOLVE THE GRISLIEST MURDER I'D SEEN.

DID DOLPH THINK LESS OF ME FOR PLAYING GROSS-OUT WITH DETECTIVE MERLIONI?

YOU KNOW WHAT TO DO WITH IT.

YEAH, HE'S IN THE KITCHEN. YOU'RE BOTH ASSHOLES, BUT IT WAS ENTERTAINING.

DID YOU GIVE MERLIONI ONE, TOO?

BUT A STUPID BET WITH MERLIONI HAD HELPED GET US ALL THROUGH THE CRIME SCENE. DARK HUMOR IS A SURVIVAL SKILL.

GIVE IT THE OLD COLLEGE TRY, EH?

WIN ONE FOR THE GIPPER.

YOU GO VISIT THE MORGUE WITH VOODOO JOHN. WE'LL TURN THIS NEIGHBORHOOD UPSIDE DOWN.

NICE TO KNOW WE'VE BOTH GOT OUR DAYS PLANNED.

DON'T FORGET, THIS AFTERNOON WE CHECK OUT SALVADOR'S HOUSE.

YEAH, AND TONIGHT WE HUNT ZOMBIES.

ANITA, WE'RE GOING TO END THIS SHIT TONIGHT.

I HOPE SO.

YOU GOT A PROBLEM WITH OUR PLANS?

JUST THAT NO PLAN IS PERFECT.

WISH THIS ONE WAS.

ME, TOO.

I USED TO COME TO THE MORGUE FAIRLY REGULARLY, TO STAKE SUSPECTED VAMPIRE VICTIMS SO THEY WOULDN'T RISE AND FEAST ON THE MORGUE ATTENDANTS.

WITH THE NEW VAMP LAWS, THAT'S MURDER. UNLESS THEY'VE SIGNED A WILL STRICTLY FORBIDDING COMING BACK AS A VAMPIRE.

MY WILL SAYS TO PUT ME OUT OF MY MISERY IF THEY THINK I'M COMING BACK WITH FANGS. HELL, MY WILL ASKS FOR CREMATION. I DON'T WANT TO COME BACK AS A ZOMBIE, EITHER, THANK YOU VERY MUCH.

MR. BURKE, HOW'S IT GOING AT YOUR SISTER-IN-LAW'S?

BLEAK, VERY BLEAK.

JOHN BURKE WAS AS I REMEMBERED HIM: TALL, DARK, HANDSOME, VAGUELY VILLAINOUS. IT WAS THE LITTLE GOATEE THAT DID IT.

THE GUARD STATION LOOKED LIKE A WWII BUNKER. THE MACHINE GUNS WERE IN CASE THE DEAD SHOULD RISE ALL AT ONCE AND MAKE FOR FREEDOM. IT HAD NEVER HAPPENED IN ST. LOUIS, BUT HAD HAPPENED AS CLOSE AS KANSAS CITY.

HI, FRED, LONG TIME NO SEE.

A MACHINE GUN WILL TAKE THE STARCH OUT OF ANY WALKING DEAD. YOU'RE ONLY IN TROUBLE IF THERE ARE A LOT OF THEM. IF THERE'S A CROWD, YOU'RE PRETTY MUCH COOKED.

I WISH THEY LET YOU COME DOWN HERE LIKE BEFORE. WE'VE HAD THREE GET UP THIS WEEK AND GO HOME. CAN YOU BELIEVE THAT?

VAMPIRES?

WHAT ELSE? THERE'S GOING TO BE MORE OF THEM THAN US SOMEDAY.

WE'RE HERE TO SEE THE PERSONAL EFFECTS OF PETER BURKE. SERGEANT RUDOLPH STORR WAS SUPPOSED TO CLEAR IT.

HE WAS PROBABLY RIGHT.

IF JOHN WASN'T INVOLVED WITH DOMINGA SALVADOR, I WOULD OWE HIM A BIG APOLOGY. BUT HOW WAS I SUPPOSED TO GET HIM TO TALK WITH DR. MARIAN HOVERING AROUND?

I HAVE TO BE HERE TO MAKE SURE NO EVIDENCE IS TAMPERED WITH. WE'VE HAD A FEW VERY DETERMINED REPORTERS LATELY.

BUT I'M NOT A REPORTER.

YOU'RE NOT AN OFFICIAL PERSON, ANITA. NEW RULES FROM ON HIGH THAT NO NONOFFICIAL PERSON IS TO BE ALLOWED TO LOOK AT MURDER EVIDENCE WITHOUT SOMEONE TO WATCH THEM.

I APPRECIATE IT BEING YOU, MARIAN.

I WAS HERE ANYWAY. I FIGURED YOU WOULD RESENT MY LOOKING OVER YOUR SHOULDER LESS THAN ANYONE ELSE.

SHE WAS RIGHT. WHAT DID THEY THINK I WAS GOING TO DO, STEAL A BODY? IF I WANTED TO, I COULD EMPTY THE DAMN PLACE AND GET EVERY CORPSE TO PLAY FOLLOW THE LEADER.

PERHAPS THAT WAS WHY I NEEDED WATCHING.

I DON'T MEAN TO BE RUDE, BUT COULD WE GET ON WITH THIS?

SURE, JOHN, WE'RE BEING THOUGHTLESS.

YOUR FORGIVENESS, MR. BURKE.

DON'T YOU THINK IF IT COULD BE ANYTHING ELSE I WOULDN'T SAY IT?

DO YOU THINK I ENJOY LEARNING MY BROTHER TOOK PART IN HUMAN SACRIFICE?

DID PETER HAVE TO BE THERE? HE COULDN'T HAVE JUST BOUGHT IT AFTERWARDS?

NO!

WHAT DOES THE GRIS-GRIS DO?

IT ENABLES A LESS POWERFUL NECROMANCER TO RAISE OLDER DEAD, TO BORROW THE POWER OF A MUCH GREATER NECROMANCER.

HOW BORROW?

THAT CHARM HOLDS SOME OF THE POWER OF THE MOST POWERFUL AMONG US. PETER PAID DEARLY, SO HE COULD RAISE MORE AND OLDER DEAD.

PETER-- GOD, HOW COULD YOU?

HOW POWERFUL WOULD YOU NEED TO BE TO SHARE YOUR POWER LIKE THIS?

IS THERE ANY WAY TO TRACE IT BACK TO THE PERSON WHO MADE IT?

VERY POWERFUL.

YOU DON'T UNDERSTAND, ANITA. THAT THING IS A PIECE OF SOMEONE'S POWER. IT IS ONE REMAINING SUBSTANCE OF WHAT SOUL THEY HAVE LEFT.

IT MUST HAVE BEEN GREAT NEED OR GREAT GREED THAT CAUSED HIM TO DO IT. PETER COULD NEVER HAVE AFFORDED IT. NEVER.

CAN IT BE TRACED BACK?

YES. JUST GET IT IN THE ROOM WITH THE PERSON WHO TRULY OWNS IT AND THE THING WILL CRAWL BACK TO HIM. IT'S A PIECE OF HIS SOUL GONE MISSING.

WOULD THAT BE PROOF IN COURT?

IF YOU COULD MAKE THE JURY UNDERSTAND IT, YES, I GUESS SO.

WHY, YOU KNOW WHO DID THIS?

MAYBE.

WHO, TELL ME WHO?

I'LL DO BETTER THAN THAT. I'LL ARRANGE FOR YOU TO COME ON A SEARCH OF THEIR HOUSE.

THE CUT WAS VERY DEEP. IT SEVERED MUSCLES IN THE NECK AND THE CAROTID ARTERY. DEATH WAS FAIRLY QUICK.

PROFESSIONALLY DONE.

WE FOUND A BODY, BUT WAS IT THE BODY WE WERE LOOKING FOR?

WELL, YES, WHOEVER CUT HER THROAT KNEW WHAT THEY WERE DOING.

THERE ARE A DOZEN DIFFERENT WAYS TO INJURE THE NECK THAT WON'T KILL OR WON'T KILL QUICKLY.

ARE YOU SAYING THAT MY BROTHER HAD PRACTICE?

I DON'T KNOW.

DO YOU HAVE HER PERSONAL EFFECTS?

RIGHT HERE.

HOW DID YOU KNOW ABOUT THE CHARM AND THE DEAD WOMAN?

I TOOK SOME EVIDENCE TO A CLAIRVOYANT. HE SAW THE WOMAN'S DEATH AND THE BRACELET.

WHAT'S THAT GOT TO DO WITH PETER?

I BELIEVE A VOODOO PRIESTESS HAD PETER RAISE A ZOMBIE. IT GOT AWAY FROM HIM. IT'S BEEN KILLING PEOPLE.

TO HIDE WHAT SHE'S DONE, SHE KILLED PETER.

WHO DID IT?

I HAVE NO PROOF UNLESS THE GRIS-GRIS WILL BE PROOF ENOUGH.

A VISION AND A GRIS-GRIS.

HARD SELL TO A JURY.

I KNOW. THAT'S WHY WE NEED MORE EVIDENCE.

A NAME, ANITA, GIVE ME A NAME.

ONLY IF YOU SWEAR NOT TO GO AFTER HER UNTIL THE LAW HAS ITS CHANCE. ONLY IF THE LAW FAILS. PROMISE ME.

I GIVE YOU MY WORD.

I DON'T TRUST JUST ANYBODY'S WORD.

WE GLARED AT EACH OTHER BUT HE NEVER FLINCHED. EITHER MY HARD-AS-NAILS LOOK HAD FADED A LITTLE, OR...

...OK, MAYBE HE MEANT TO KEEP HIS WORD.

ALRIGHT, I'LL TAKE YOUR WORD. DON'T MAKE ME REGRET IT.

I WON'T. NOW GIVE ME THE NAME.

EXCUSE US, MARIAN. THE LESS YOU KNOW ABOUT ALL THIS, THE GREATER YOUR CHANCES OF NEVER WAKING TO A ZOMBIE CRAWLING THROUGH YOUR WINDOW.

VERY WELL, BUT I WOULD DEARLY LOVE TO HEAR THE COMPLETE STORY SOMEDAY, IF IT'S SAFE.

IF I CAN TELL IT, IT'S YOURS.

YELL WHEN YOU'RE FINISHED. I'VE GOT WORK TO DO.

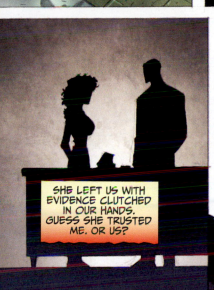

DOMINGA SALVADOR.

SHE LEFT US WITH EVIDENCE CLUTCHED IN OUR HANDS. GUESS SHE TRUSTED ME. OR US?

I KNOW THAT NAME. SHE IS A FRIGHTENING FORCE, IF ALL THE STORIES ABOUT HER ARE TRUE.

THEY'RE TRUE.

YOU'VE MET HER?

I'VE HAD THE MISFORTUNE.

I DIDN'T LIKE THE LOOK ON HIS FACE.

YOU SWORE NO REVENGE.

THE POLICE WILL NOT GET HER. SHE IS TOO CRAFTY FOR THAT.

WE CAN GET HER LEGALLY. I BELIEVE THAT.

BUT YOU AREN'T SURE.

WHAT COULD I SAY? HE WAS RIGHT.

I'M ALMOST SURE.

ALMOST IS NOT GOOD ENOUGH FOR KILLING MY BROTHER.

THAT ZOMBIE HAS KILLED A LOT MORE PEOPLE THAN JUST YOUR BROTHER. I WANT HER, TOO.

BUT WE'RE GOING TO GET HER *LEGALLY*, THROUGH THE COURT SYSTEM.

THERE ARE OTHER WAYS TO GET HER.

IF THE LAW FAILS US, FEEL FREE TO USE VOODOO. JUST DON'T TELL ME ABOUT IT.

NO OUTRAGE ABOUT ME USING BLACK MAGIC?

THE WOMAN TRIED TO KILL ME ONCE. I DON'T THINK SHE'LL GIVE UP.

YOU SURVIVED AN ATTACK BY THE SEÑORA?

I CAN TAKE CARE OF MYSELF, MR. BURKE.

I DON'T DOUBT THAT, MS. BLAKE.

I'VE BRUISED YOUR EGO. YOU DON'T LIKE ME BEING SO SURPRISED, DO YOU?

KEEP YOUR OBSERVATIONS TO YOURSELF, OKAY?

IF YOU HAVE SURVIVED A HEAD-ON CONFRONTATION WITH WHATEVER DOMINGA SALVADOR SENT AFTER YOU, THEN I SHOULD HAVE BELIEVED SOME OF THE STORIES I HEARD ABOUT YOU.

THE EXECUTIONER, THE ANIMATOR WHO CAN RAISE ANYTHING NO MATTER HOW OLD.

DOMINGA SALVADOR, THE PERFECT PICTURE OF MATERNAL BLISS. I WANTED TO THROW UP.

OF COURSE, JUST BECAUSE SHE WAS THE MOST DANGEROUS VOODOO PRIESTESS I'D EVER MET DIDN'T MEAN SHE WASN'T A GRANDMA, TOO. PEOPLE ARE SELDOM JUST ONE THING.

HITLER LIKED DOGS.

YOU ARE MORE THAN WELCOME TO SEARCH, SERGEANT. MY HOUSE IS YOUR HOUSE.

MRS. SALVADOR, DO YOU UNDERSTAND THE POSSIBLE IMPLICATIONS OF THIS SEARCH?

THERE ARE NO IMPLICATIONS BECAUSE I HAVE NOTHING TO HIDE.

ANITA, MR. BURKE.

I BELIEVE YOU KNOW MS. BLAKE.

I HAVE HAD THE PLEASURE.

THIS IS JOHN BURKE.

SO GLAD TO MEET YOU AT LAST, MR. JOHN BURKE.

ALWAYS GOOD TO MEET ANOTHER PRACTITIONER OF THE ART.

DO IT, ANITA.

WHAT IS THAT?

COME NOW, SEÑORA, DO NOT PLAY THE FOOL. YOU KNOW VERY WELL WHAT IT IS.

I KNOW THAT IT IS A CHARM OF SOME KIND, OF COURSE. DO THE POLICE NOW THREATEN OLD WOMEN WITH VOODOO?

WHATEVER WORKS.

ANITA.

SORRY.

IF THIS WORKED AND IF WE COULD GET IT ADMITTED INTO COURT, AND IF WE COULD EXPLAIN IT TO THE JURY, THEN WE MIGHT HAVE A CASE.

HOW MANY IFS IS THAT?

TO BE CONTINUED!

in Anita Blake, The Laughing Corpse — Executioner